YOU GOT THIS THING

Jossea K. Rilea

Published by The Place of Wonder

Registered in New York

www.theplaceofwonder.com

ISBN #978-1-935734-45-1

Disclaimer: The content in this book is intended for entertainment purposes only and is not intended as, nor should it be considered a substitute for, professional medical advice, diagnosis or treatment.

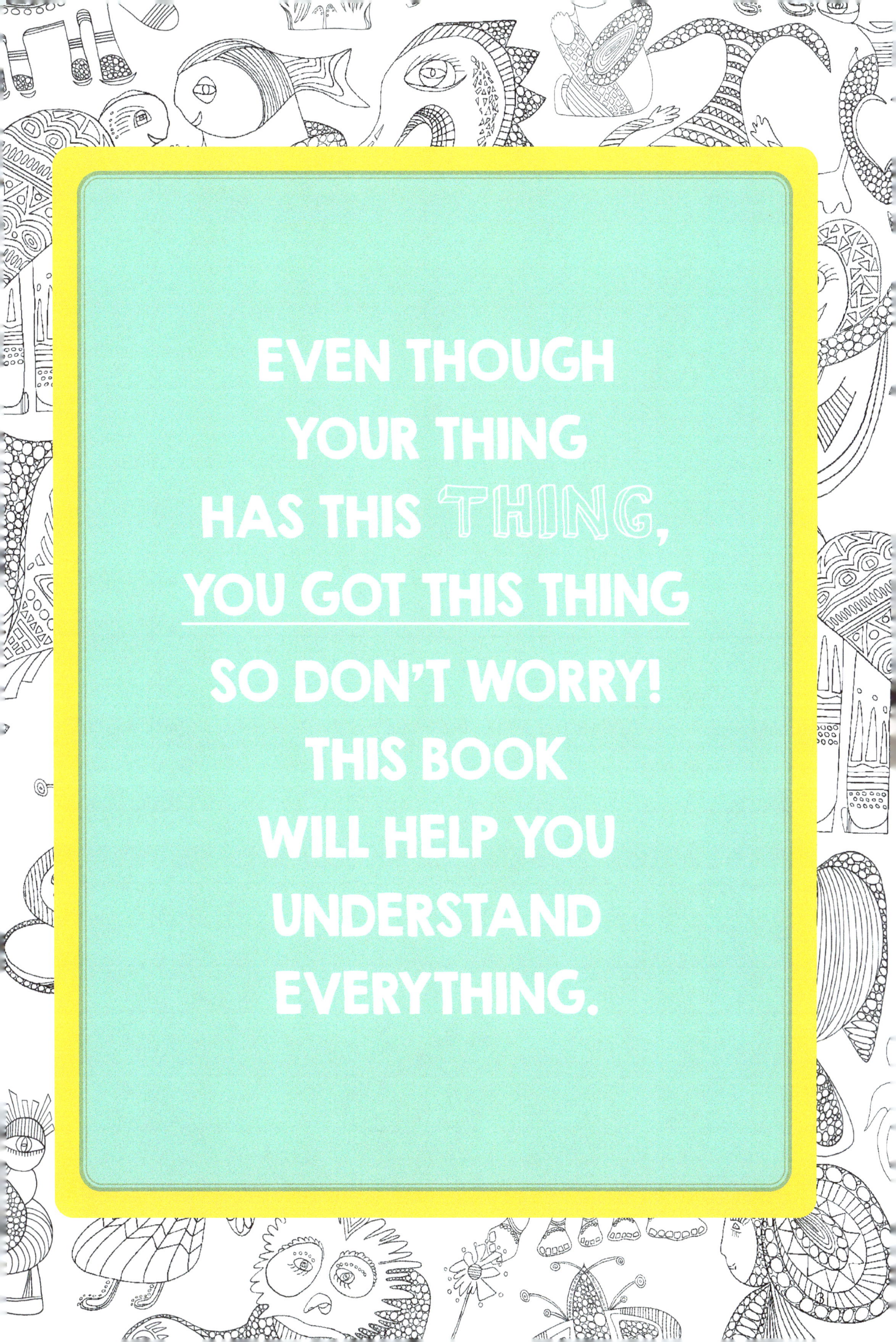

EVEN THOUGH
YOUR THING
HAS THIS THING,
YOU GOT THIS THING
SO DON'T WORRY!
THIS BOOK
WILL HELP YOU
UNDERSTAND
EVERYTHING.

CONGRATS! YOUR THING CHOSE YOU!

Caretaker
(Your name)

____

The "Thing" That Your Thing Has
(Anything you live with and take care of —Any ailment, disability, disease, disorder, illness, injury, syndrome, etc.)

____

Your Thing's New Name
(Fill this in after reading page 46)

____

Date You Met Your Thing
(Date of your diagnosis)

____

GETTING TO KNOW YOUR THING

To make sure your Thing gets the care and attention it needs, you first have to get to know it a little better. That's what this book is all about.

Once you get to know your Thing, you'll discover that it's much easier to take care of than you thought in the beginning. Your doctors and nurses will explain how to take care of it, but you'll be its best friend and caretaker—*24 hours a day, seven days a week*—and it will depend on you for a lot of things. Don't worry if you don't know what to do at first. Feeling like this is completely normal. The good news is, you'll never be alone! Throughout this book, you'll meet lots of Things who will give you tips on how to take care of <u>your</u> Thing.

After spending a lot of time getting to know your Thing, you'll find out that it is one-of-a-kind—*just like you*—and you'll soon be an expert at taking care of it. Ready to get started?

9

MEET: **IZAR**
LEARN: How to give your Thing the care and attention it needs

IZAR

17

MEET: **ORI**
LEARN: How to feed your Thing

ORI

25

MEET: **GEMMA**
LEARN: How to travel with your Thing

GEMMA

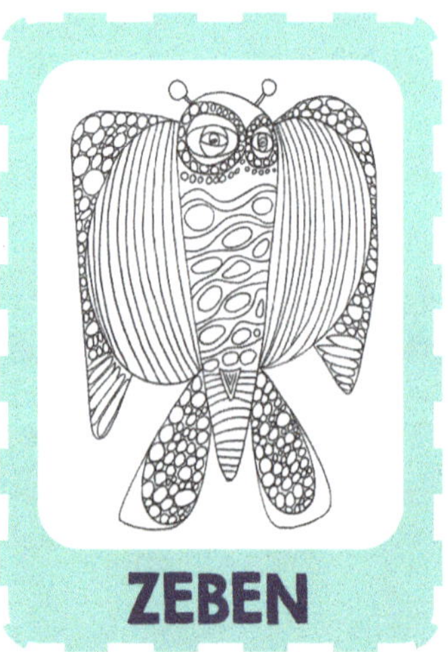

31

MEET: **ZEBEN**
LEARN: How to encourage your Thing to chill out

ZEBEN

39

MEET: **LEONIS**
ART PROJECT:
What does your
Thing look like?

LEONIS

49

MEET: **DENAB**
LEARN: How to
become best friends
with your Thing (even
if you don't like each
other at first)

DENAB

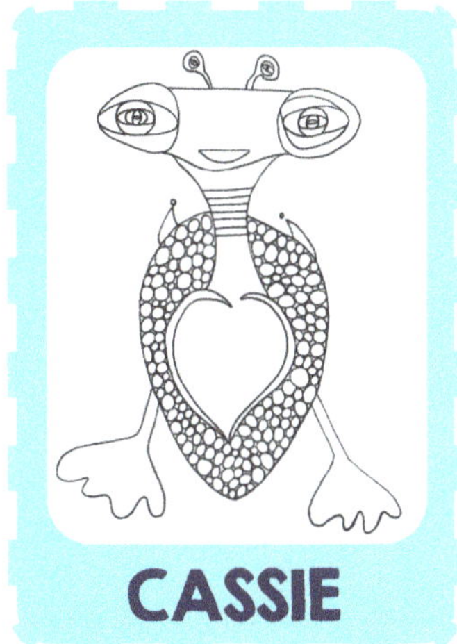

57

MEET: **CASSIE**
LEARN: How to
lull your Thing
to sleep

CASSIE

63

MEET: **PERSIE**
LEARN: How to
cheer up your
Thing

PERSIE

71

MEET: **ZOSMA**
LEARN: How to
forgive your Thing

ZOSMA

79

MEET: **CEPHIE**
LEARN: How to
imagine the best for
your Thing

CEPHIE

87

MEET: **ETA**
LEARN: How to
celebrate every
day with your
Thing

ETA

THIS BOOK can be read in any order.
You can start on page 9 or page 49. To help
you remember which pages you want to revisit,
write your favorite page numbers here:

I LOVE PAGES...

COSMIC CARE
with IZAR

COSMIC NAME:
IZAR

FROM THE STAR CONSTELLATION:
VOLANS

LOVES: FISHING, PLAYING TENNIS and SKIPPING ROCKS

How to give your Thing the care and attention it needs

NO TWO THINGS ARE THE SAME. You will know best how to take care of yours, but here are a few caretaking tips :

Trust yourself. When taking care of your Thing, one of the most important things you can do is *trust yourself.* When you do, you'll know when something doesn't feel right and can ask for help.

Check in with your Thing every day. How's your Thing feeling? Ask yourself if there's anything else you can do to make it feel better.

Be kind to yourself. Sometimes there's nothing more that can be done to help your Thing besides what you're already doing. You're doing the best that you can.

Anticipate change. What your Thing needs one day might not be what it needs the next. Think of every day as an adventure.

Embrace your "new normal." Focus on what's ahead—there's a lot to look forward to! When you focus on what is, instead of what's is not, things may start to feel less overwhelming.

Nobody knows your Thing like you do! List the ways you like to take care of your thing:

1.

2.

3.

Read, read, read. Write three sentences about what you've learned about your Thing—things your doctor told you or things you've read online.

1.

2.

3.

Talk to others. Write a list of support groups in your area as well as websites that you trust where you can go for advice and support.

____
____
____
____
____
____
____
____

Build a support team. Don't be afraid to ask for help from your family and friends. Write a list of people you can count on during an emergency as well as their contact information. Be sure to let them know they are on your list and how they can help. Mostly, thank them for being there for you.

NAME	CONTACT INFORMATION

QUESTIONS TO ASK YOUR DOCTORS

Q: ____

A: ____

Q: ____

A: ____

Q: ____

A: ____

Q: ____

A: ____

LIST OF MEDICATIONS

Name	For What?	Dose	Directions	Doctor's Name

UPCOMING APPOINTMENTS

Date: _____________________

Time: _____________________

Location: _____________________

Date:_____________________

Time: _____________________

Location: _____________________

Date: _____________________

Time: _____________________

Location: _____________________

Date:_____________________

Time: _____________________

Location: _____________________

Date: _____________________

Time: _____________________

Location: _____________________

Date:_____________________

Time: _____________________

Location: _____________________

Date: _____________________

Time: _____________________

Location: _____________________

Date: _____________________

Time: _____________________

Location: _____________________

Date: _____________________

Time: _____________________

Location: _____________________

Date: _____________________

Time: _____________________

Location: _____________________

Date: _____________________

Time: _____________________

Location: _____________________

~ THOUGHTS ~

How ya doing?
Can I help with anything?

COSMIC NUTRITION
with ORI

COSMIC NAME:
ORI

FROM THE STAR CONSTELLATION:
PAVO

LOVES: MARBLES, COLLECTING ROCKS and FUNNY MOVIES

How to feed your Thing

CHANGE YOUR WORDS CHANGE YOUR WORLD

What kinds of thoughts and ideas do you feed your Thing every day? It's normal for a lot of thoughts to run through your mind. But have you ever noticed if these thoughts are positive or negative? Using the spaces on the next page, write down any negative thoughts you say to (or about) your Thing. Don't judge what you hear. Then, see if you can turn these thoughts into positive ones.

EXAMPLE:

Negative thought: *"I hate having to take care of my thing every day!"*

Give it a + twist: *"Despite the fact that I have to take care of this Thing, I have a lot to offer the world and I love who I am."*

Since you can't change the fact that your Thing exists, all you can do is change the way you think about it. After a month of changing your words, notice if you can see any positive changes in your world.

Here's a fun way to see what kind of "photos" you're invisibly sharing with yourself. Take one of your negative thoughts and draw a picture of it on the left side. Then make that same sentence positive and draw a new image of it on the right. Which one of these pictures is the kind of photo you would share or like online?

Draw your negative thought:	**Draw your positive thought:**

CAN YOU SHIFT YOUR THOUGHTS FROM NEGATIVE TO POSITIVE?

Negative thought: ____
Give it a + twist: ____

Negative thought: ____
Give it a + twist: ____

Negative thought: ____
Give it a + twist: ____

Negative thought: ____
Give it a + twist: ____

Negative thought: ____
Give it a + twist: ____

Negative thought: ____
Give it a + twist: ____

Negative thought: ____
Give it a + twist: ____

Negative thought: ____
Give it a + twist: ____

Negative thought: ____
Give it a + twist: ____

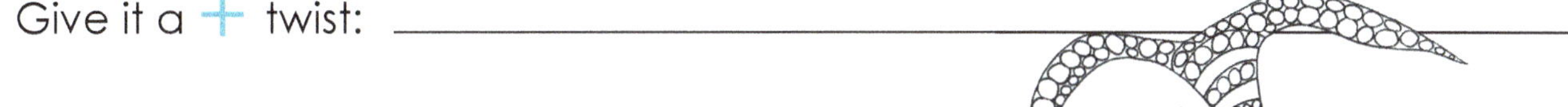

Negative thought: ____
Give it a + twist: ____

Negative thought: ____
Give it a + twist: ____

Negative thought: ____
Give it a + twist: ____

FEED YOUR THING GOOD THOUGHTS EVERY DAY
SMILE
LOVE
GIVE
LAUGH
TRUST
SHARE
ACCEPT
MAKE
DREAM

(REAL) FOOD LIST

Have you been told by your doctors to feed your Thing certain foods and avoid others? Write a list of foods that your Thing can't eat in the "no" column and a list of foods that it can in the "yes" column. *Always consult a nutritionist or doctor before making changes to your diet.*

"NO" FOODS   **"YES" FOODS**

~ THOUGHTS ~

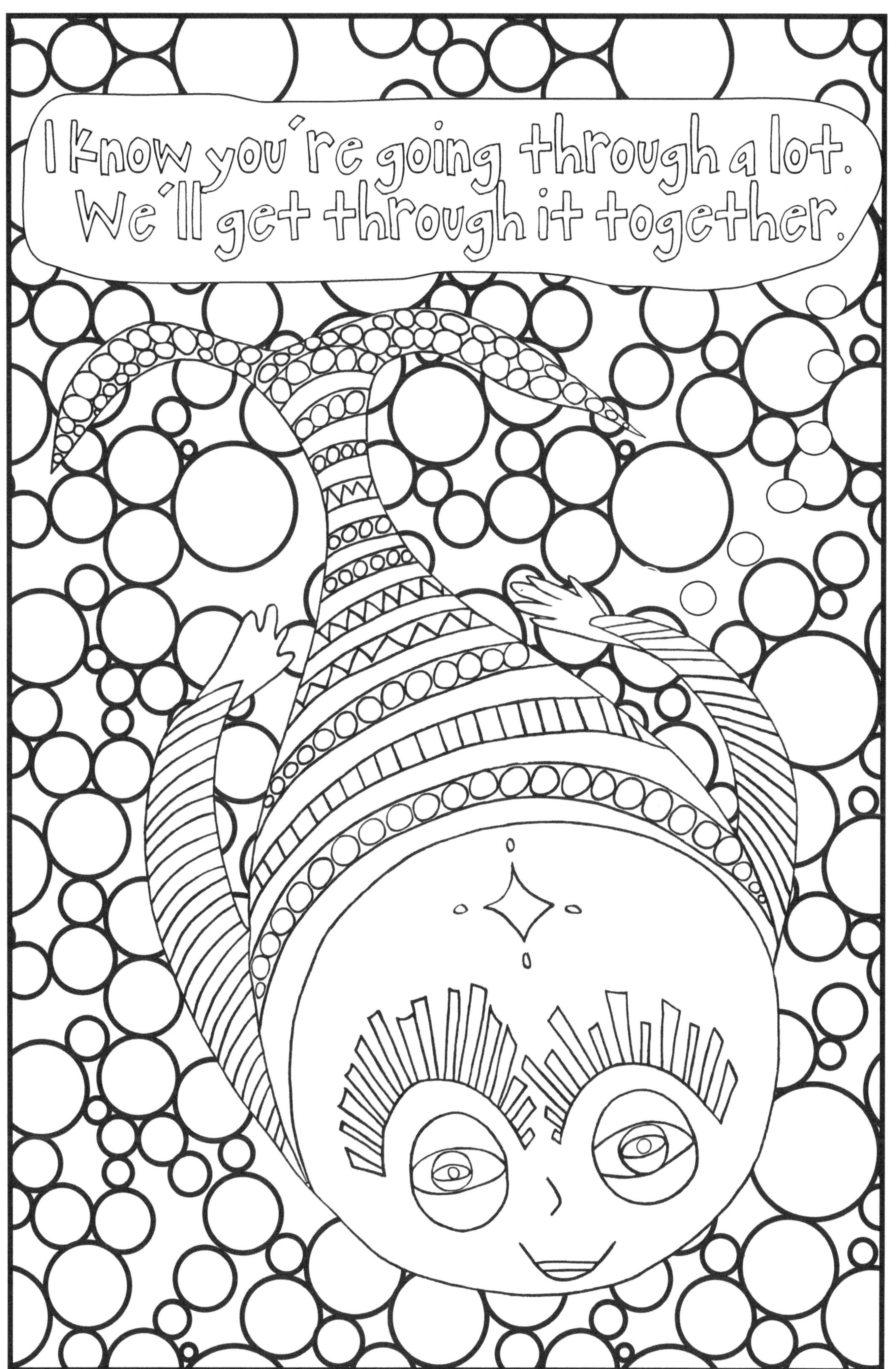

I know you're going through a lot.
We'll get through it together.

COSMIC TRAVELING
with GEMMA

COSMIC NAME:
GEMMA

FROM THE STAR CONSTELLATION:
LEPUS

LOVES: WINTER, WRITING NOTES and DAYDREAMING

How to travel with your Thing

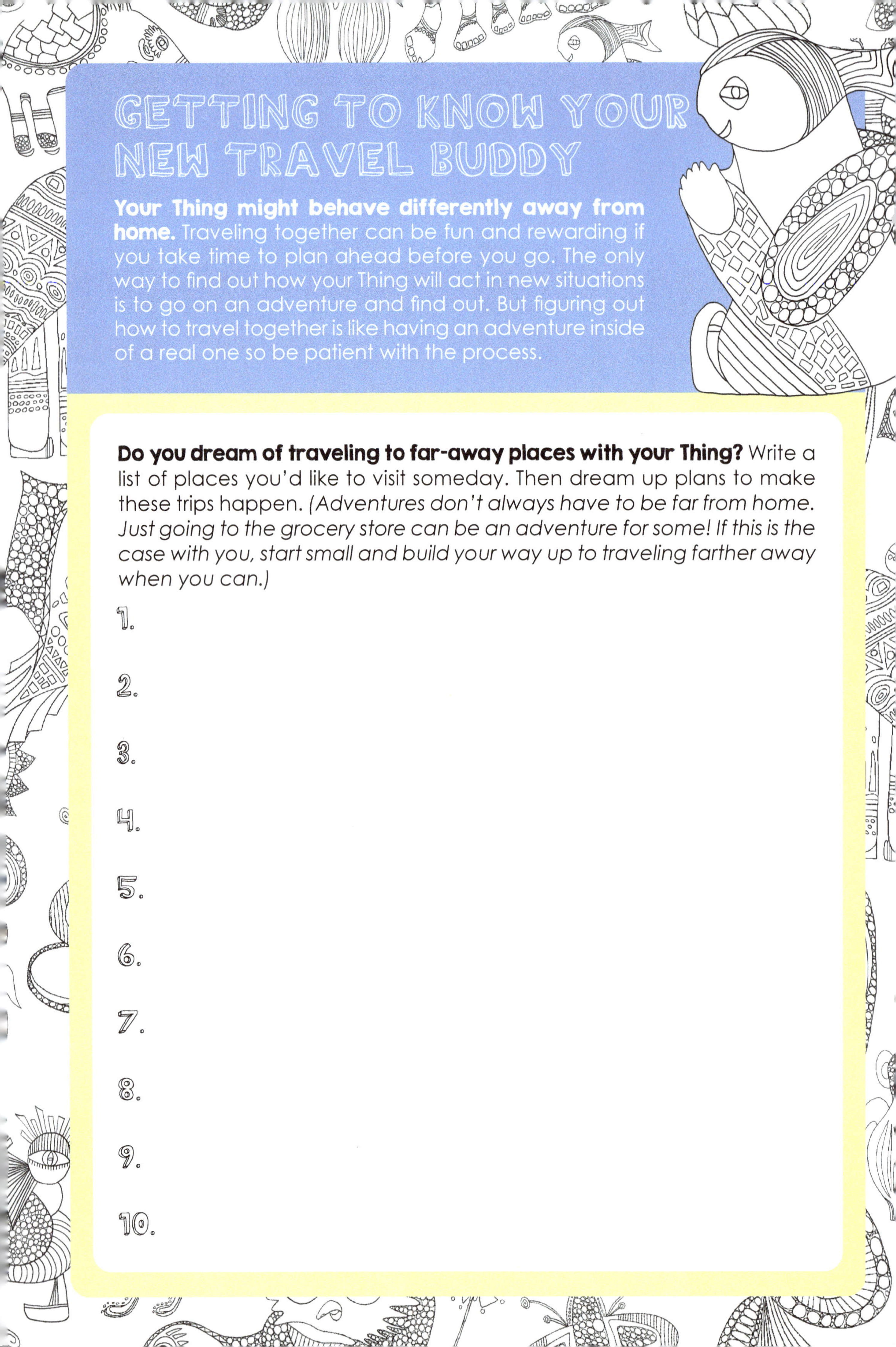

Your Thing might behave differently away from home. Traveling together can be fun and rewarding if you take time to plan ahead before you go. The only way to find out how your Thing will act in new situations is to go on an adventure and find out. But figuring out how to travel together is like having an adventure inside of a real one so be patient with the process.

Do you dream of traveling to far-away places with your Thing? Write a list of places you'd like to visit someday. Then dream up plans to make these trips happen. *(Adventures don't always have to be far from home. Just going to the grocery store can be an adventure for some! If this is the case with you, start small and build your way up to traveling farther away when you can.)*

1.

2.

3.

4.

5.

6.

7.

8.

9.

10.

TRAVELING TIPS:

- Until you know how your Thing will be able to handle the stress of traveling, give yourself extra time to get where you're going in case you need to take frequent rest breaks.
- Go into every new situation with a positive attitude.
- If your Thing is sensitive and gets sensory overload around loud noises, bright lights and busy crowds, consider packing ear plugs, calm music, sunglasses and a hat.
- Be patient with your Thing and give it time to adjust to new environments and situations.
- Be sure to pack a few of your favorite foods so that your Thing can enjoy something familiar while away.
- Rest before you leave so you're ready to have fun when you arrive.

IMPORTANT DOCUMENTS:

In case you need to go to a doctor or hospital while traveling, be sure to have your insurance card, the names and phone numbers of your home doctors and a list of medications that you take all written down on one sheet of paper. This way, you won't have to remember everything in your head and can easily give this paper to anyone who needs it.

Visualize your upcoming trip before you go so you'll have confidence that your trip will be a success. Before you leave, imagine your entire trip in your mind—from start to finish—to make sure you've thought of everything you might encounter while away. Then write a list of challenges you think you'll have to overcome. Finally, tell yourself that no matter what happens, you're going to have fun and enjoy yourself.

____

____

____

____

____

____

____

____

PACKING LIST

You can do this. I believe in you.

COSMIC COURAGE
with ZEBEN

COSMIC NAME:
ZEBEN

FROM THE STAR CONSTELLATION:
HYDRA

LOVES: QUIET TIME, LANDSCAPING and DANCING

How to encourage your Thing to chill out

DIVE INTO YOUR SENSES

There are many unknowns when it comes to taking care of a Thing and so it's normal to have anxiety at times. These feelings are usually not permanent. Over time, things should settle down because you'll have a better understanding of how to take care of your Thing. In the meantime, the best way to calm anxiety, fear or stress is to *get moving*. Dive into the physical world so you're not thinking too much.

Exercise is one way to do this but you can also try putting your phone away and enjoying the tactile, real world.

Try some of these fun activities or invent your own:

- Redecorate your room or rearrange your furniture
- Build something with your hands like a bird box or an origami fish
- Go "forest bathing" and walk through the woods looking for treasures
- Walk barefoot in the grass or build a mini-house for a small creature
- Paint rocks, balance rocks or throw rocks in a pool of water
- Build a sand castle, then knock it down and build another one

What are some other ways you can dive into your senses?

____

____

TAPPING TRICK

One of the most effective and easiest ways to reduce fear & anxiety quickly is to TAP on a meridian point on the back of your hand. This simple technique involves tapping with 3 fingers on the "gamut point." The next time you feel stress popping up, TAP this spot and see what happens. How do you feel? Has your fear lessened? If this works for you, you can search for "EFT Tapping" online and learn more simple techniques.

Place 3 fingers on the 3 dots (on either hand) and gently tap for 30 seconds or more.

CAN YOU IMAGINE YOUR FEARS GETTING SMALLER?

In the first frame, draw a picture of something you're afraid of. Next, draw this same fear in the second frame, only this time draw it smaller. Then draw your fear getting smaller and smaller in all of the remaining frames. How do you feel at the end?

You can repeat this exercise in your mind as many times as you need to using your imagination.

RELEASE YOUR FEARS

What are you afraid of? Another way to let go of your fears is to write them down with as many details as possible. After you're done, ask yourself if they're as scary as you thought they were when they were stuck in your head.

DRAW A PICTURE OF YOURSELF
SURROUNDED BY POSITIVE
IMAGES AND WORDS

COLORING IS CALMING

Try it out the next time you need to relax

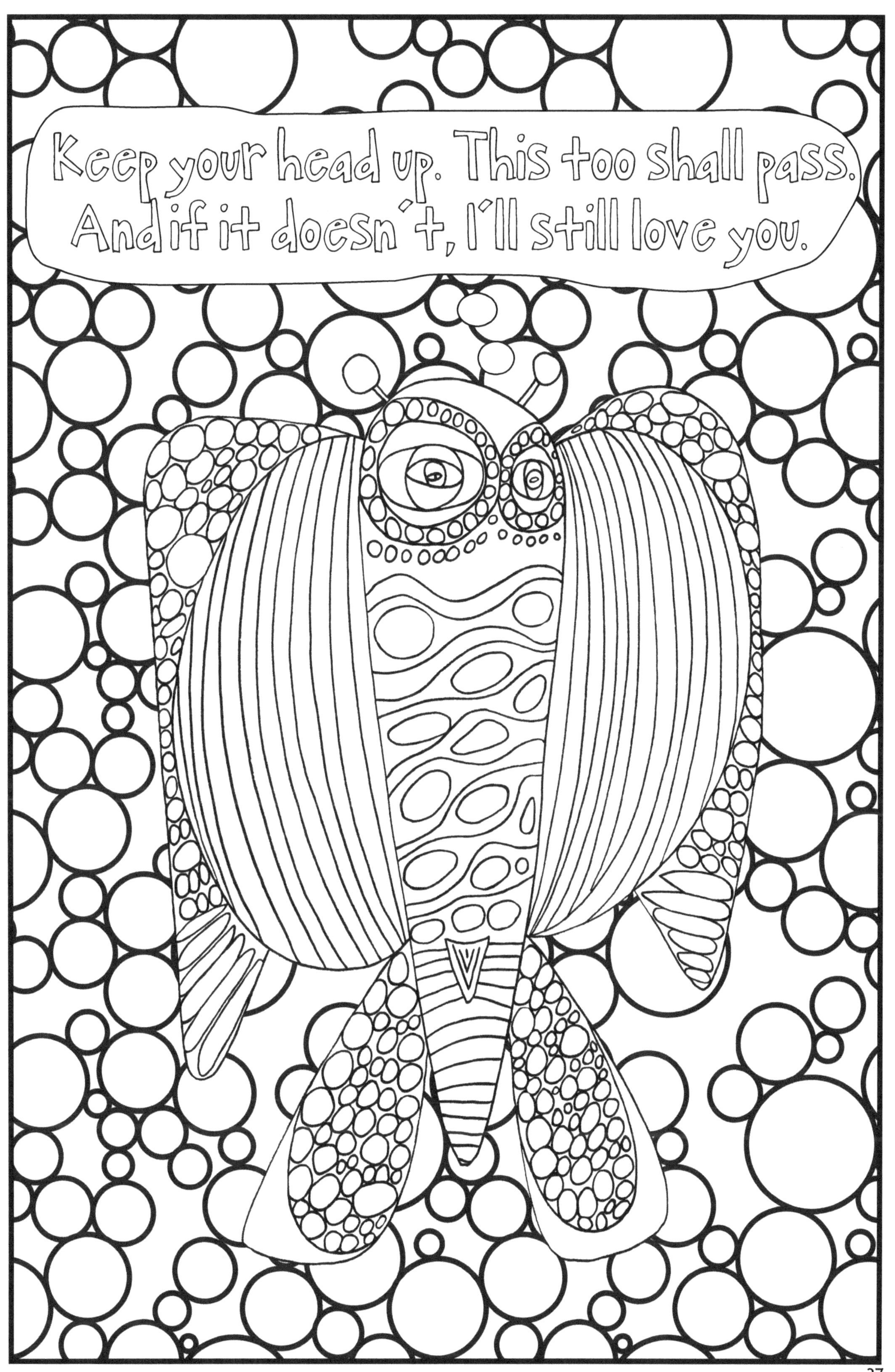

Keep your head up. This too shall pass.
And if it doesn't, I'll still love you.

COSMIC ART PROJECT
with LEONIS

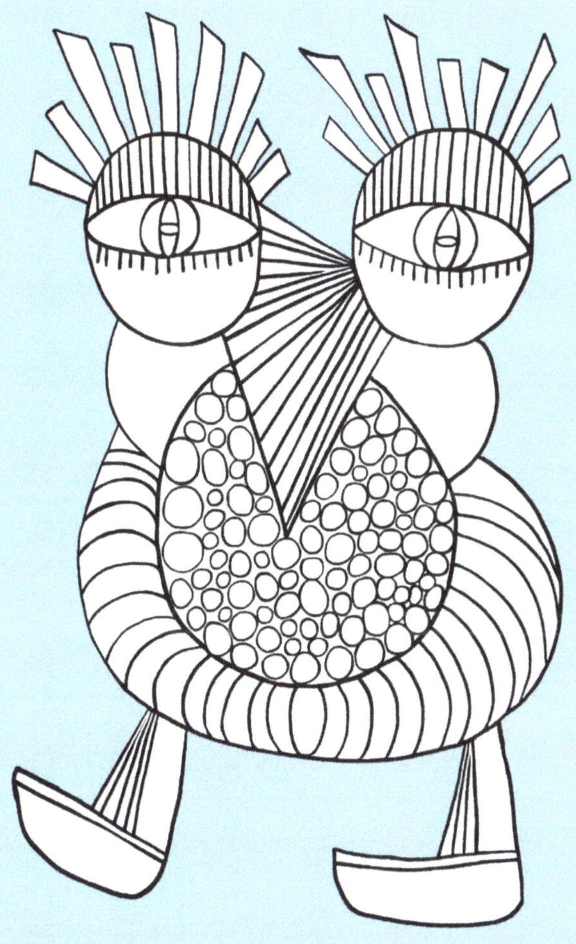

COSMIC NAME:
LEONIS

FROM THE STAR
CONSTELLATION:
CRATER

LOVES: APPLES,
FAST PLANES
and TIME TRAVEL

What does your Thing look like?

ART PROJECT

What does your Thing look like?

To draw your Thing, follow these steps:

STEP 1: Write a list of your symptoms in the box below and imagine how you might draw them.

STEP 2: Imagine a lovable, cosmic creature in your mind.

STEP 3: Imagine what this creature would look like if it had all of your symptoms—*This is your Thing!*

STEP 4: Draw a picture of your Thing on the blank pages that follow. If you take care of more than one, draw those, too.

STEP 5: Take a photo of your Thing.

STEP 6: If inspired, share your drawing on social media as a way to inspire others.

Your artwork will bring HOPE, LOVE and JOY to those who need it the most.

LIST YOUR SYMPTOMS	IDEAS ON HOW TO DRAW THEM
1.	1.
2.	2.
3.	3.
4.	4.
5.	5.
6.	6.
7.	7.

NEED IDEAS ON HOW TO DRAW YOUR SYMPTOMS?

If you're not sure how to begin to imagine what your Thing looks like, visit www.theplaceofwonder.com to see what others have drawn.

Here are some tips on how to draw your symptoms:

Feeling tired?

Maybe your Thing has sloth toes or sleepy eyes.

Have a headache?

Maybe you could draw your Thing with a really big head because that part of your body seems to be all you worry or think about.

Do your muscles ache? Are you in pain?

Perhaps your Thing has bulging muscles that look bigger than they actually are since they take up so much space in your mind.

Have a stomachache?

Maybe you could draw your Thing with a giant stomach or maybe you could draw a zoo inside your stomach because it grumbles and growls all the time.

Feeling dizzy?

Maybe your Thing is tipped over or slanted or off balance.

There are no wrong ways to draw your Thing. Whatever pops into your mind is the right way!

Sometimes, having to explain your Thing to others is one of the hardest parts about having one!

Drawing and sharing a photo of your Thing might make it easier for you to explain it to others so they can better understand what you're going through.

I GOT THIS THING

I GOT THIS THING

I GOT THIS THING

I GOT THIS THING

RENAMING YOUR THING

Now that you've drawn a picture of your Thing, and you know what it looks like, you're ready to give it a new name.

Cosmic Name:

____

From the Star Constellation:

____

Loves:

____

Write a short story about your Thing

Need inspiration? Visit www.theplaceofwonder.com to read about other Things.

____
____
____
____
____
____
____
____

Nobody else might understand but I do. I feel your pain.

COSMIC FRIENDSHIP
with DENAB

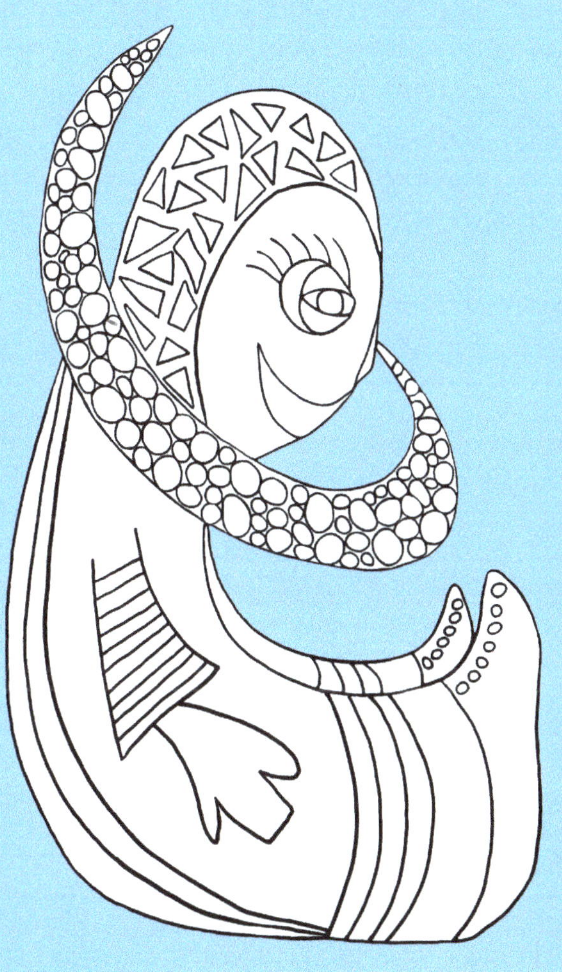

COSMIC NAME:
DENAB

FROM THE STAR CONSTELLATION:
CETUS

LOVES: LAUGHING, RIDING A BIKE and DRAWING

How to become best friends with your Thing (even if you don't like each other at first)

CELEBRATE EVERYTHING THAT MAKES YOU UNIQUE

In order to become best friends with your Thing, you must first become best friends with yourself. An important thing to always remember is that you are not your Thing! So, who are you, then?

"Who you are" is not just what you do. For example, you may like to play soccer or you may like to read books but that is not who you are, that's just what you like to do. "Who you are" goes deeper than this—it's who you are on the inside. You might be creative and kind. Perhaps you are a helper or someone who can make others laugh. Not sure who you are? What does everyone else see and love about you? This is who you are.

In this space, write an honest and true description of yourself.

IMAGINE YOUR DREAM LIFE

You and your Thing will become best friends once you realize that you can have big dreams despite having to take care of it. Write a description of what you'd like your dream life to look like... together.

____

____

____

____

____

____

____

____

____

____

____

____

____

____

____

COMPASSION + UNDERSTANDING

Living with a Thing can be unpredictable. Sometimes you'll make plans and then your Thing will start acting up and ruin them. Although this might be a challenge, in the moment when your plans are changed, try to remember that today is today but tomorrow is tomorrow and you can always try again then. Treat your Thing the same way you would treat a good friend, with compassion and understanding.

DREAM BIG! LIST YOUR TOP 10 DREAMS AND GOALS.

1.

2.

3.

4.

5.

6.

7.

8.

9.

10.

KEEP GOING. THE SKY IS THE LIMIT. LIST 10 MORE.

1.

2.

3.

4.

5.

6.

7.

8.

9.

10.

~ THOUGHTS ~

I think you're amazing
no matter how you're feeling.

COSMIC DREAMS
with CASSIE

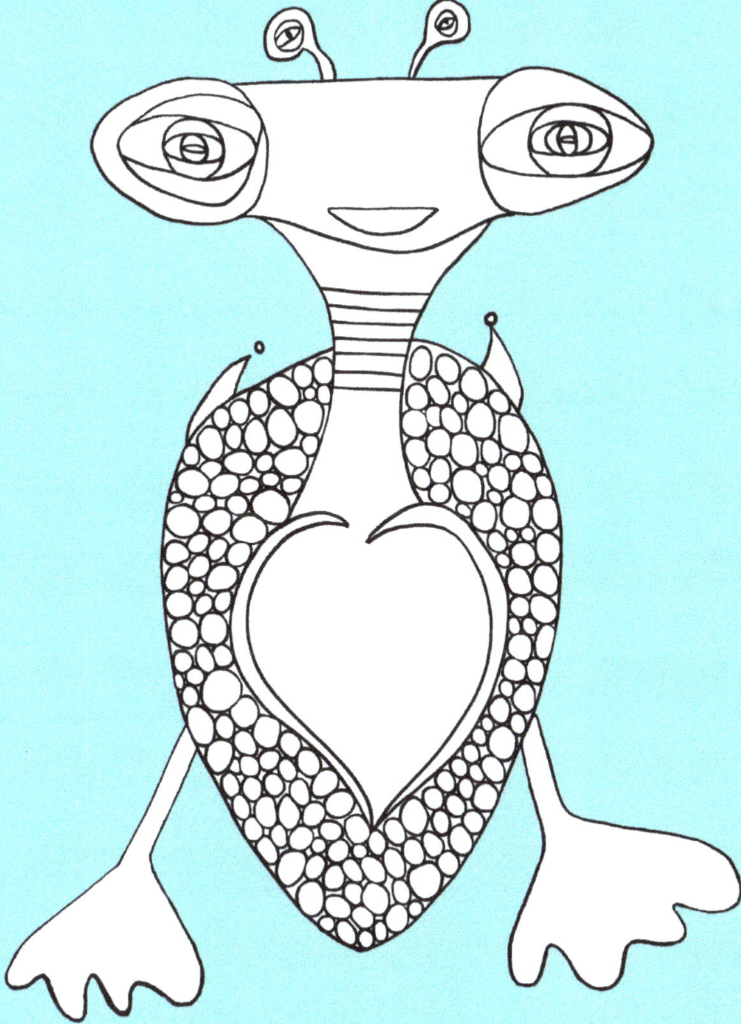

COSMIC NAME:
CASSIE

FROM THE STAR CONSTELLATION:
PICTOR

LOVES: UNICORNS, TREE HOUSES and WEARING HATS

How to lull your Thing to sleep

WHAT DO YOUR DREAMS MEAN?

Everyone dreams at night. Can you remember if any of these images have popped into one of your dreams? If so, circle them. Do any of them have a special meaning in your life? What do they mean to you?

Jewels   Dove   Clock   Ocean   Lake

Door   Knots   Dancing

Bird   Colors   Animals   City   Unicorn

Stairs   Garden   Dog   Dolphin   Keys

Horseshoe   Clouds   Cave

Boat   Butterfly   Sun

Island   Earth   Hat

Ice Cream   Egg   Rabbit

Hero   Bottle

Elephant   Mountain

Plant   River   Grass   Moon

Ring   Music

Jungle   Wings   Mermaid

Tree   Orchestra   Night

Mandalas   Water

Whale   Wheel

Road   Shell   Train

Door   Ship   Planet

UFO

Sky   Shoe   Star   Frog   Book

SWEET DREAMS MEDITATION

One way to help your Thing fall asleep is to lie in a quiet room and imagine it in your mind. Then, imagine your Thing getting comfortable in its favorite sleeping spot. Imagine it lying down, curling up and about to go to sleep. Then imagine that you're guiding your Thing in a meditation to help it fall asleep, almost like you are reading it an invisible bedtime story.

Silently, in your mind, say, "Relax your feet. Relax your ankles. Relax your calves. Relax your knees. Relax your legs. Relax your belly. Relax your chest. Relax your neck. Relax your head. Relax your whole body. Good night, Thing. Sweet dreams."

THE PLACE OF WONDER

Your dreams are a place where you can connect directly with your Thing. That's because your Thing and your dreams both exist in your imagination, inside the place of wonder—the place we all go when we dream.

HOW TO REMEMBER YOUR DREAMS

The best way to remember your dreams is keep this book and a pen next to your bed so you can write down your dreams as soon as you wake up. When writing, see if you can remember any colors, shapes, ideas, people, objects or feelings. Write down as many details as possible, along with the date and time when you had the dream. What does your dream mean to you?

____

____

____

____

____

____

____

____

____

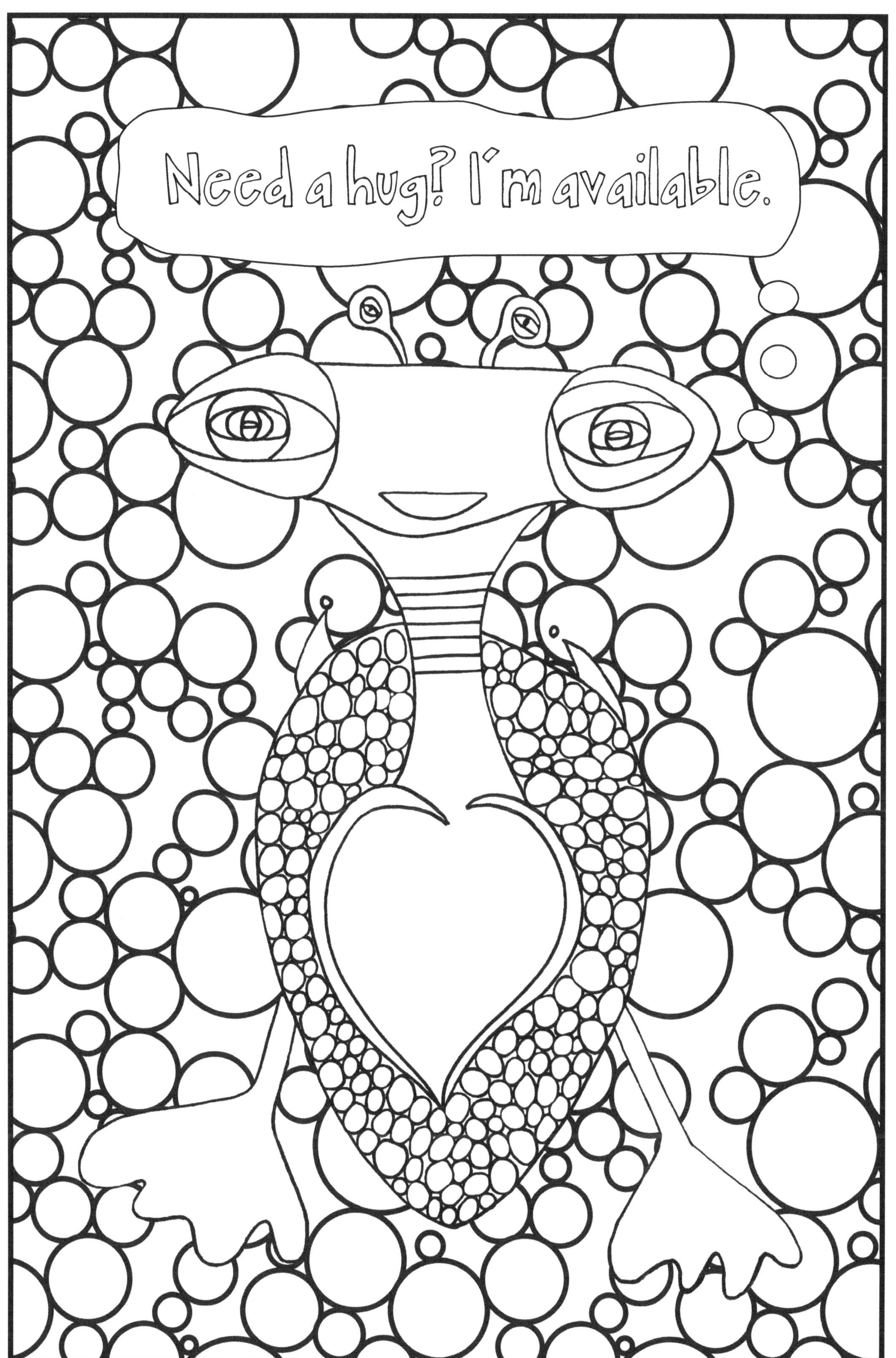
Need a hug? I'm available.

COSMIC FEELINGS
with PERSIE

COSMIC NAME:
PERSIE

FROM THE STAR CONSTELLATION:
OCTANS

LOVES: ACTING, THE COLOR BLUE and ROAD TRIPS

How to cheer up your Thing

FOLLOW THE (GOOD) FEELINGS FOLLOW YOUR HEART

Taking care of a Thing 24 hours a day, seven days a week can sometimes make you forget all of the things that make you feel good. But chances are, when you're happy, your Thing will be, too! In this space, write about what makes your heart sing.

DRAW A PICTURE OF SOME OF YOUR FAVORITE THINGS

BUILD A GRATITUDE BANK

 Write a list of everything that you're grateful for. Anytime you're feeling sad, upset or angry you can read your list to remind yourself of all the good things in your life.

1.

2.

3.

4.

5.

6.

7.

8.

9.

10.

11.

12.

IT'S OKAY TO FEEL ALL KINDS OF EMOTIONS

Cherish your good days and accept the bad days. Just because you have to take care of a Thing doesn't mean you have to be sad and depressed. It's okay to have fun and enjoy yourself—*even on your bad days!* It's normal to have good days when you're feeling great and bad days when you don't feel like doing much of anything. This is important for your friends and family to understand. You can let yourself play, find joy, laugh, smile and do things that bring happiness into your life, regardless of whether you are having a good day or a bad day.

WRITE A LIST OF EVERYTHING THAT MAKES YOU SMILE

1.

2.

3.

4.

5.

6.

7.

8.

9.

10.

11.

12.

13.

14.

15.

16.

17.

18.

19.

20.

WRITE A STORY ABOUT
YOUR HAPPIEST MEMORY

~ THOUGHTS ~

Sometimes life is not kind.
I hear ya. I'm listening.

COSMIC FORGIVENESS
with ZOSMA

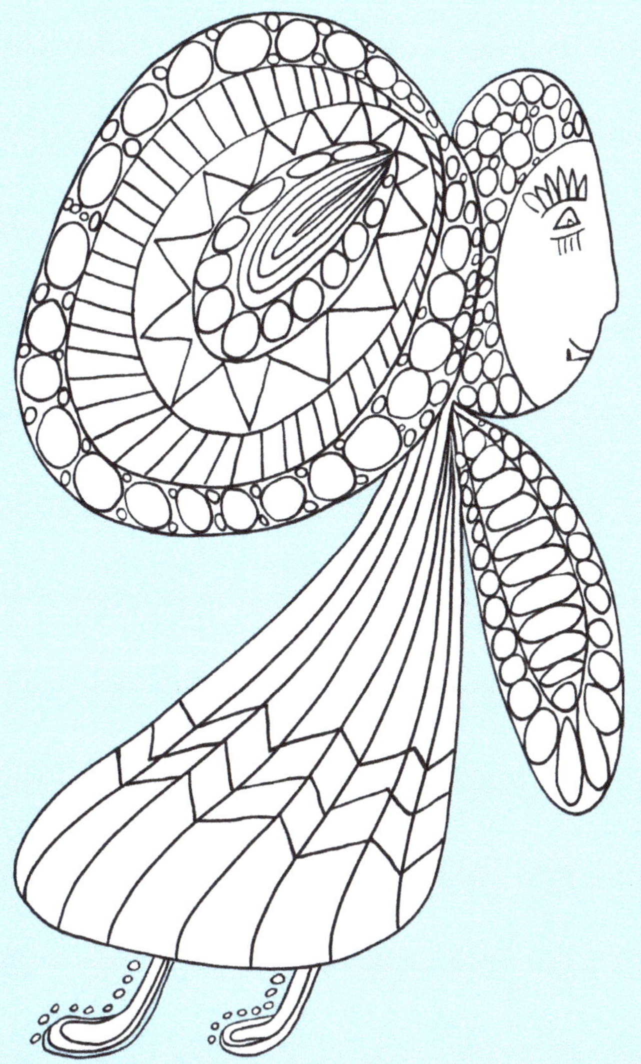

COSMIC NAME:
ZOSMA

FROM THE STAR
CONSTELLATION:
CIRCINUS

LOVES: FLYING,
BIRTHDAY PARTIES,
and DREAMING

How to forgive your Thing

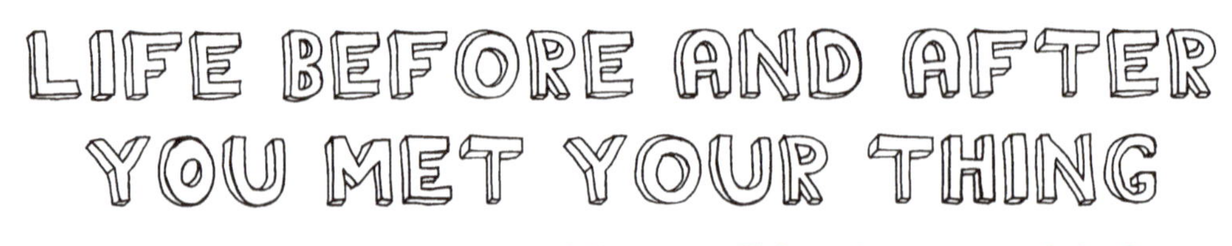

LIFE BEFORE AND AFTER YOU MET YOUR THING

If you met your Thing at age 5 or 10 or 15 or 25, you can probably remember what life was like before the "big meeting." If this is the case with you, acknowledging that things have changed is a big step in moving foward and creating your "new normal" life... full of all of the wonderful things you love! But before you can fully move forward, it's helpful to look back and process all that has changed. This process might make you feel a little sad at first. Even though it might be hard right now, grieving your old life will make it easier to move forward in the future.

To start the process, write down everything that is different in your life now that you have to take care of your Thing. Try to be as honest as possible.

____

____

____

____

____

____

____

____

____

____

____

____

____

IT'S NOT YOUR FAULT

It's not your fault that you have to take care of your Thing. It's just the way things happened in your life. There's no way to go back in time to before you met each other. The best way to move forward is to forgive your Thing so space is opened up for joy and happiness to enter your life.

FORGIVENESS POEM

Write a poem (or a letter) to your Thing

____

____

____

Does it feel good to forgive your Thing?

ANGER IS A NORMAL EMOTION

On a day when you're feeling upset, come back to this page
and write down everything that's making you feel that way.

SCRIBBLE AS FAST AS YOU CAN
ALL OVER THIS PAGE

GO AHEAD. LET IT ALL OUT.
DON'T HOLD BACK.

~ THOUGHTS ~

You're never alone.
I'm always here for you.

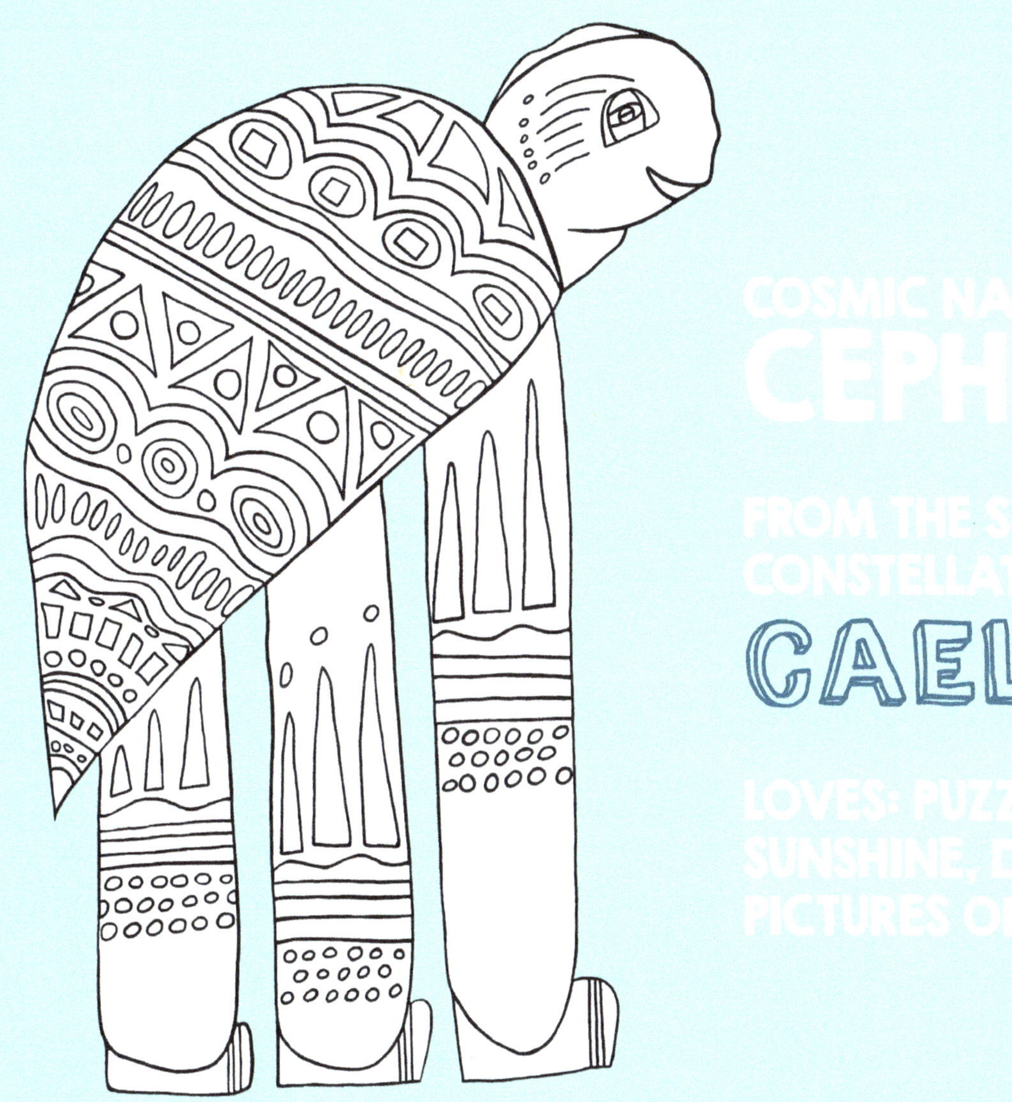

COSMIC NAME:
CEPHIE

FROM THE STAR
CONSTELLATION:
CAELUM

LOVES: PUZZLES,
SUNSHINE, DRAWING
PICTURES OF FISH

How to imagine the best for your Thing

WRITE AND DIRECT YOUR OWN INVISIBLE MOVIE

Dreams that you have while you're sleeping are like secret invisible movies only you can see. Dreams that you have while you're awake are also invisible but they're different because you're actively creating them using your own imagination. You can either imagine a story that someone else has written or you can imagine your own stories. When you imagine your own ideas, you become the writer and director of your own invisible movie.

Have you ever wondered if you could make your Thing feel better just by using your imagination? In the invisible world, anything is possible. It is a gigantic space full of endless possibilities.

On a day when you're not feeling so great and don't feel like doing much of anything else, see if you can imagine a movie in your mind where your Thing starts to feel better.

There aren't any rules in the invisible world but this will help get you started:

1. Close your eyes. Pretend you're watching the beginning countdown of a movie — 3, 2, 1 — and imagine seeing white numbers appear on a black background.
2. On a blank screen, watch as your movie begins and your Thing appears. What does it look like? How big is it? What color is it? What is it doing? Allow all of the images to appear without forcing them. Just watch what appears with no judgement, as if you were watching a movie.
3. Next, see if you can imagine your Thing transforming. As an active participant in your own movie, you can decide what to imagine and what this dream looks like. How would you make your Thing feel better if you could use anything in the whole universe (real or imagined) to make it happen? There are no limitations to what you can dream up. Try to imagine this movie in great detail and take your time. If you're not sure how you'd begin to make your Thing feel better, ask your Thing to make itself feel better for you.

There's no wrong way to make an invisible movie. Notice if you are watching a movie or if you are creating one. Which do you like better? Some of both? Can you make the movie change? It can be a lot of fun to explore all of the ways that your Thing can transform just by using your imagination.

MAKE AN INVISIBLE MOVIE

If your Thing could star in its own invisible movie, what would it be called and what would happen in the movie to make your Thing feel better?

Invisible Movie Title:

INVISIBLE MEDICATION

Using your imagination is a powerful tool you can use when you feel like there's nothing else you can do to help your Thing feel better.

- Where is your favorite place (real or imagined) to go to relax? Is there a place that feels safe and healing to you? Imagine this place in your mind every time you feel scared or overwhelmed. How does it make you feel to imagine visiting this place with your Thing?

- What color would you choose to describe one of your Thing's symptoms? Imagine scanning your Thing's body to look for that color. Then, once you find the color, imagine using a giant eraser to erase it. For example: Let's say your Thing has a headache. Imagine that the headache is the color blue. Then, imagine looking at your Thing's head, seeing a spot of blue and erasing it with a giant eraser. Does that makes the headache go away?

- If you have a fever, imagine slowly moving a piece of ice over your Thing's forehead to cool it down.

- Does your Thing have any tension in its body? How would you release it? Would you unbutton it? Unlock it? Loosen it?

- Imagine that a rocket ship or alien spaceship takes your Thing's pain away, deep into space, so that it never returns ever again.

- Like roots under a tree, imagine that your Thing's symptoms go directly into the earth under your feet and disappear.

- Imagine a ball of bright light in your hands. Then, imagine holding this ball of light over the part of your Thing's body that hurts. As the light shines down on your Thing, imagine the light washing away your Thing's symptoms.

- Imagine shining sunlight from a special flashlight into any part of your Thing's body where there's any kind of pain. Does the sunlight make the pain go away?

- Want to have some fun? How about throwing an invisible party to celebrate all of the healthy cells in your Thing's body.

The possibilities for creative visualization are endless because your imagination has no limits. On the next page, see if you can come up with your own invisible medication.

INVISIBLE MEDICATION LIST

Using your own ideas, see if you can dream up your own unique invisible "medicines" to lessen your Thing's symptoms. It's always best for you to imagine your own ideas that have personal meaning to you when helping your Thing.

Symptom: ____

Invisible medication: ____

Symptom: ____

Invisible medication: ____

Symptom: ____

Invisible medication: ____

Symptom: ____

Invisible medication: ____

Symptom: ____

Invisible medication: ____

Symptom: ____

Invisible medication: ____

Symptom: ____

Invisible medication: ____

Symptom: ____

Invisible medication: ____

Symptom: ____

Invisible medication: ____

Symptom: ____

Invisible medication: ____

Symptom: ____

Invisible medication: ____

~ THOUGHTS ~

Invisible pain is the pits. I've got it, too. I'm like really? Seriously?

COSMIC CELEBRATION
with ETA

COSMIC NAME:
ETA

FROM THE STAR CONSTELLATION:
ANTLIA

LOVES: WATER, STORYTELLING and SUMMERTIME

How to celebrate every day with your Thing

CELEBRATE YOUR ACCOMPLISHMENTS

Take time to acknowledge how far you've come.

Come back to this page in one week, one month or one year and write down everything you're proud of achieving.

____

____

____

____

____

____

____

____

KEEP MOVING FORWARD

In the upcoming weeks, months and years you'll have to give your Thing more care and attention than you've ever given anything else in your life. Remember to read this book again from time to time to remind yourself of everything that you've learned.

The more you learn about and practice the ideas in this book, the more confident you'll be in your ability to take care of your Thing. So, hang in there, keep your chin up and always remember...

YOU GOT THIS THING!

Certificate of
ACHIEVEMENT
Awarded To
For successfully completing the
You Got This Thing training course
Signed By
Date
YAY!
You're on your way!

~ THOUGHTS ~

Today is a new day. No matter what's happening, let's find something to celebrate!